ON THE LINE

BY JAKE MADDOX

illustrated by Sean Tiffany

text by Bob Temple

Librarian Reviewer
Chris Kreie
Media Specialist, Eden Prairie Schools, MN
M.S. in Information Media, St. Cloud State University, MN

Reading Consultant
Mary Evenson
Middle School Teacher, Edina Public Schools, MN
M.A. in Education, University of Minnesota

STONE ARCH BOOKS
Minneapolis   San Diego

Jake Maddox Books are published by Stone Arch Books,
A Capstone Imprint
1710 Roe Crest Drive
North Mankato, Minnesota 56003
www.capstonepub.com

Library of Congress Cataloging-in-Publication Data
Maddox, Jake.

On the Line / by Jake Maddox; illustrated by Sean Tiffany.

p. cm. — (Jake Maddox Books. A Jake Maddox Sports Story)

Summary: After breaking his arm during the first day of try-outs
last season, Robby is determined to make the football team this year,
but to do so he must face his own fears and the bully who tackled him
the year before.

ISBN-13: 978-1-59889-062-4 (library binding)

ISBN-10: 1-59889-062-X (library binding)

ISBN-13: 978-1-59889-240-6 (paperback)

ISBN-10: 1-59889-240-1 (paperback)

[1. Football—Fiction. 2. Self-confidence—Fiction. 3. Bullies—
Fiction. 4. Teamwork (Sports)—Fiction.] I. Tiffany, Sean, ill. II. Title.
III. Series: Maddox, Jake. Impact Books (Stone Arch Books) Jake
Maddox Sports Story.
PZ7.T2438On 2007
[Fic]—dc22   2006006079

Art Director: Heather Kindseth
Cover Graphic Designer: Heather Kindseth
Interior Graphic Designer: Kay Fraser

Printed in the United States of America in Stevens Point, Wisconsin.
052013
007383R

TABLE OF CONTENTS

Chapter 1

BAD MEMORIES

Robby Samuels stood on the hill next to his school. He looked down at the green football fields below.

As he stood there, he remembered every second of last year's football season. That was easy to do, since his season lasted about twenty minutes. In the first contact drill of tryouts, Robby fell and broke his arm. Now he couldn't get that moment out of his head.

His job was to block a defensive player. He had looked across the line at the player he was supposed to block. It was Andy Renkins, one of the best football players in the league.

"Good luck," Andy had said to Robby, sarcastically. "Try not to hurt yourself."

Then the coach's whistle sounded. Andy pushed him aside like he was brushing away an insect. Andy stood over Robby, holding the ball. "Football's a man's game," Andy said. "Looks like you better try something else."

Now Robby wasn't sure that playing football was his dream anymore. He certainly looked like a football player. His thick chest and strong, muscular legs made him look tough, even if he didn't feel that way.

Even though everybody got to be on a team, the coaches held tryouts to figure out who the best players were. That way, they could divide them up between the teams.

"You better get down there," Matt said. Matt, Robby's best friend, was a year younger and a lot smaller than Robby. He didn't like sports, but he was always there for Robby.

"You're right," Robby said. He took a deep breath, but his legs didn't move.

"Go!" Matt said. "This is a new year. Stop thinking about your arm. And stop thinking about stupid old Andy Renkins!"

Finally, Robby trudged down the hill toward tryouts and Andy Renkins.

Chapter 2

TRYOUTS

Most of the players were in the main field, stretching out. Robby sat in the middle, hoping to disappear. It only took a minute for Andy Renkins to spot him.

"Well, look who's back!" Andy said. "Think you'll make it to the second day of tryouts this year, Samuels?"

Robby didn't say anything. He'd learned a long time ago to ignore Andy.

When the boys were done stretching, the coach blew his whistle. "Break into your groups! Group A, you're doing sprints! Group B, you're blocking and tackling!"

Robby was in Group B. He looked around quickly for Andy. Then Robby saw him, heading over to the sprint station with Group A. Robby relaxed.

Robby got down into his stance, facing Seth Wilson. He didn't care that Seth was bigger than he was. As long as he didn't have to block Andy.

The coach blew his whistle. Robby held Seth off for a couple of seconds before Seth overpowered him and got the ball.

"Good job, both of you!" the coach shouted. "That was quite a battle."

Quite a battle. To Robby, those words meant everything. His chest puffed out under his pads.

His next battle was against Ryan Swanson, a boy about Robby's size. This time, Robby was trying to get to the ball. When the whistle blew, Robby charged at Ryan. Their shoulder pads hit with a loud clap.

"Woooo-hoooo!" the coaches howled. Robby kept charging ahead. In a flash, he was on the ball.

Robby felt a rush of emotion. It was a feeling he'd never had before. Then coach blew his whistle. "Rotate!" he yelled.

Robby jogged toward the next station, sprints. He felt great out there on the field, actually competing in football.

Just then, he felt his shoulder jerk back. His feet lifted off the ground. He looked up and saw Andy standing over him.

"Keep your head up, Samuels!" Andy laughed. "You're going to hurt yourself!"

Chapter 3

GETTING THE NEWS

Robby picked himself off the field and moved to the next station. He wished he had gotten back up and slammed back into Andy.

The tryouts continued for three days. Each day, the players did drills at different stations. Coaches from all the teams watched and made notes about the players on their clipboards.

At the end of the third day, Robby stopped by Matt's house on the way home.

He needed to do something a little less active than play football. He invited Matt over to play Galactic Meltdown.

That night, in the middle of the video game, the phone rang at Robby's house. Robby ignored it. A second later, his mom walked into the room with the phone.

"For me?" The only person who ever called him was Matt, and Matt was sitting next to him.

Robby took the phone.

"Robby," Coach Parker said. "You're going to play for the Lions. After watching you in tryouts, I think we're going to have you play on the line.

"I just e-mailed the roster to your parents," the coach continued. "Take a look at our team. I think we're going to be pretty good!"

Robby thanked the coach and rushed into the family room. His team's roster was already on the computer screen. Robby's eye went to one name, right above his: Renkins, Andy.

Chapter 4

PRACTICE TIME

The next afternoon, all the boys on Robby's team met for their first practice. The boys tossed footballs and did stretching exercises.

"Bring it in, boys," the coach barked. They gathered around Coach Parker. The coach's son, James, stood next to him.

"I'm Coach Parker," he said.

"I've been coaching in this league for a long time. Last year, my team won the championship. I expect to do the same thing this year."

The team perked up.

"Winning is hard work," the coach continued. "Each of you has to learn your position and do your job the right way. If we all work together, we will win the championship!"

Now the boys were excited. Robby felt it too.

After that, the coach ran the team through drills. The toughest drill had two players against each other in a narrow space. One player ran the ball, while the other player tried to tackle him.

One small boy named Michael had never played football before. He was afraid of getting hit hard. When he got the ball, he would wait to be tackled.

"Michael!" the coach yelled. "Don't wait for the tackler to hit you! Run him over!"

Robby didn't mind the drill. He was usually pretty good at the tackling part, unless the player was really fast.

Andy Renkins was good at all of it. Andy usually tackled the player before he could get past the line of scrimmage. When Andy had the ball, he ran over smaller players and faked out bigger ones.

The coach's son, James, was a good player too.

Toward the end of practice, the coach held one more round of the tackling drill. When it was Michael's turn to carry the ball, the coach called his son over. He spoke to him quietly.

He's probably telling James to take it easy on Michael, Robby thought.

When it came time for the players to line up, however, something very different happened. James got down into his defensive stance. Michael stood five yards away with the ball in his hand. He looked scared.

Bleet! went the coach's whistle. Michael never moved. Before he had a chance, James barreled toward him. Michael was knocked straight back.

The rest of the players were silent, but the coach went crazy.

"Yeahhhh!" screamed Coach Parker. "That's the kind of hit we need. Make him remember you!"

James got up. Andy ran over and gave him a high five. Michael stayed flat on his back.

"Hop up, Michael," Coach Parker said. "You just got the wind knocked out of you. You'll be fine in a second."

Michael walked off to the side of the field and sat down.

"That was a pretty good start, but we'll have to work harder if we're going to win the championship!" the coach yelled.

Suddenly, Robby wasn't sure he wanted to win a championship anymore.

Chapter 5

ATTITUDE CHANGE

Robby was worried. It was bad enough to play on the same team with Andy Renkins. Now he was starting to wonder about his coach.

One night, Matt stopped over after practice. "What are you so upset about?" Matt said.

Robby thought about it for a minute. "I'm not sure I like playing football anymore," he said.

"I can't believe you're going to let Andy and your coach wreck your season," Matt said, shaking his head. "You still like football, right?"

"Yeah, I do," Robby said. He was starting to get a little defensive. "What's your point?"

"Then go play!" Matt said. "Just because they are taking it so seriously doesn't mean you have to!"

Finally, Robby spoke. "Thanks," he said quietly.

Robby knew Matt was right.

The next night, at the beginning of practice, Coach Parker called Robby over. "Samuels, I'm making you the starting center."

Robby knew he would start every play. His job was to snap the ball between his legs to the quarterback. Then he had to block a defensive lineman.

It was important for the center and the quarterback to work well together. That way, the plays would all start smoothly. James was going to be the quarterback.

The rest of that week, Robby tried to learn his new position. His most important job was remembering the snap count.

In the huddle, the quarterback would tell the play and the snap count. "Thirty-six power right," James would say. "On two."

Usually, he would say it twice, so everyone would remember.

Then everyone would say "Ready, break!" and head to the line of scrimmage. Robby learned to repeat the snap count in his head all the way to the line. On two, on two, on two, he would think.

At the line, James would crouch behind Robby and put his hands down to receive the ball. "Down!" he would yell. "Set!"

Then came the count. "Hut! Hut!" Since the play was on two, Robby's job was to give the ball to James on the second "Hut!"

If he did it too early, the rest of the team wouldn't be ready to start the play on time. If he waited too long and the rest of the offensive players moved before the ball did, it would be a penalty.

Most of the time, Robby did just fine. Once in a while, he'd make a mistake. "Samuels!" the coach yelled when Robby messed up. "You are key to the play! Pay attention!"

As the team got closer to the start of the season, the coach got more serious. One practice, he made new rules. "From now on, when one person makes a mistake, we'll all pay the price." Some of the players groaned.

That was one of the worst practices Robby had. He messed up on the snap count twice and fumbled the ball once. Each time, Coach Parker made the team run a sprint. By the end of practice, the whole team was mad.

Andy was the maddest. "Samuels, you're a great teammate," he said. "I was really hoping to run all those extra sprints."

Robby never said anything back to Andy. In a way, Robby knew Andy was right. He decided to work harder.

Chapter 6

SCRIMMAGE

After three weeks of practice, the Lions only had one night left before their first game.

Coach Parker arranged a scrimmage against the Packers.

"This is a chance for us to see how good we really are," Coach Parker said. "We'll know what things we need to work on before the first game."

The scrimmage started out great. Robby kept his focus and remembered the snap count. He got the ball quickly into James's hands.

Andy Renkins was playing running back, so he carried the ball on most of the plays.

After ten plays, it was time for the Packers to be on offense. Robby wasn't a starter on defense, so he left the field. Robby watched from the sidelines. He looked across the field and saw Matt. He gave Robby the thumbs-up sign.

After a short break, it was the Lions' turn to go back on offense.

"I know we can do better," Coach Parker said. "Let's really take it to them this time!"

The offense ran out on the field. They got into the huddle. James called the play.

"Forty-six power sweep," he said. "On one." Then he repeated it.

As he bent over the ball, Robby's mind went blank.

Before he could do anything, James started calling out the signals. One or two? One or two? Robby kept thinking.

"Hut!" James yelled. The rest of the linemen started to block, but Robby didn't move.

The referee blew his whistle and threw his penalty flag.

"Samuels!" Coach Parker yelled. "Pay attention!"

Robby felt terrible as he went back into the huddle. James called the next play. "Forty-four power sweep," James said again. "This time, on two. Okay? Forty-four power sweep on two."

Andy stared straight at Robby. "That's two, Samuels," he said. "Got it?"

Robby was mad. Mostly, he was mad at himself. "Yeah, I got it," he said. "Don't worry. I'm not an idiot."

The rest of the players looked stunned. Robby rarely said anything during practices. Andy glared at Robby.

On the next play, James almost dropped the ball and then handed it sloppily to Andy. Andy struggled to control it. By the time he had a firm grip on it, the defense was on him.

Andy only gained two yards. Robby was knocked down by the player he was blocking. He was still getting off the ground when Andy walked by.

Just then, Robby felt a sharp pain in his right hand. "Ahhh," Robby yelped. Andy had stepped on him with his spikes.

Robby knew one thing: He wasn't going to let Andy know it hurt. Robby went back to the huddle.

But when he tried to grip the ball for the snap, he couldn't hold it tightly.

The next three snaps, Robby lost control of the ball. Coach Parker yelled at Robby each time.

After the third fumble, Coach Parker grabbed Robby by the face mask. "If you can't handle this job," he said, "I'll find someone else who can!"

Robby fought through the rest of the scrimmage without any fumbles or mistakes. After practice, Coach Parker pulled Robby aside.

"Samuels," Coach Parker said. "You'll do better next time."

"Coach, my hand got stepped on," Robby said. "That's why I was fumbling."

"Don't make excuses," the coach said. "You're going to have to work harder, that's all."

Chapter 7

GAME TIME

Robby walked home from practice with Matt.

"Tough scrimmage, huh?" Matt asked. Robby didn't say a word.

Robby wanted to do anything but talk about the scrimmage. He didn't want to even think about it.

Finally, Matt said, "Do you want to practice your snaps with me?"

"Are you serious?" Robby asked.

When they got to Robby's house, they started practicing snaps. Robby showed Matt how to hold his hands to get the ball. Matt barked out the signals, just like James did. Time after time, Robby snapped the ball straight into Matt's hands.

His hand was still hurting, but Robby wasn't going to stop. He and Matt stayed in the backyard until it was dark.

The next morning Robby felt better. That night would be the first game of the season.

The day couldn't go fast enough for Robby. As he walked into his classroom, he saw Andy Renkins sitting in the front row. "Here comes butterfingers," Andy said to one of his buddies. "Hey, Samuels, don't drop your pencil."

I'll show him tonight, Robby thought. He'll see what kind of player I really am.

Game time was six o'clock, but Robby had to be at the field an hour early for stretching and warming up.

As soon as he got to the field, his coach called him over.

"Samuels," the coach said, "I was a little hard on you last night. Your job is very important to our team. We can't win if the plays get off to a bad start."

"Don't worry, Coach. I practiced last night. I'm ready," Robby said.

The Lions were playing against the Cowboys in the first game of the season.

The Cowboys had some good players. Mike Jarvis, the player Robby would be blocking every play, was big and strong.

Soon the players huddled for their pregame pep talk. "Okay, boys," Coach Parker said. "You can't win this game by yourselves. You need your teammates."

Then he looked right at Robby. "If everyone just concentrates and does his job, everything will be okay."

Robby felt ready.

Chapter 8

KICKOFF

Before Robby knew it, it was time for the game to begin. The Lions got the ball first. Robby couldn't wait for the first offensive play of the game.

James made the call in the huddle. All Robby heard was "On two." Then James said the play again. Again, he said, "On two."

The team broke the huddle and trotted toward the line. On two, on two, on two! Robby thought.

He got to the line, crouched down, and grabbed the ball. He looked straight at Mike Jarvis. Mike was staring right back, trying to scare Robby.

Robby's eyes grew wide. He felt nervous and his mind went blank. What's the count? Robby thought. Then James started barking out the signals.

"Down!" James yelled. "Set!"

All at once, it came back to Robby in a rush. Two, he thought. It's on two.

Hut! Hut!

Robby snapped the ball and plowed into Mike Jarvis. It was a good battle, and neither player gained control. Andy got the ball from James and rushed to the ten-yard line.

"Wooo-hooo!" Coach Parker yelled from the sidelines. All of the Lions' parents went crazy. On the next play, Andy ran for the touchdown. The Lions made the extra point, and the score became Lions 7, Cowboys 0.

All the Lions' players were high-fiving and jumping on each other. "We're going to be unstoppable!" Coach Parker said.

Robby just smiled.

Chapter 9

A BIG CHANGE

The Lions' defense stopped the Cowboys on their next drive. The Lions got the ball back near midfield and scored another touchdown. Then the Cowboys got a touchdown right before halftime, making the score 14–7. At the start of the second half, the Cowboys quickly tied the game.

In the fourth quarter, the Lions got the ball inside the Cowboys' territory. One more touchdown might mean victory.

In the huddle, James called out the play. "Twenty-two power drive," James said. "On two." Robby would have to snap the ball and then control Mike Jarvis to keep him from getting Andy.

"Get it to me quick," Andy said to James. "We've got to be quick if I'm going to get through."

James nodded. The team headed for the line. Robby glanced at Mike Jarvis, and then crouched over the ball.

"Down! Set!" James barked. Andy stood in the backfield, ready for the ball. Robby was focused.

"Hut!" James cried. James shifted his feet and started to pull back. "Hut!" he screamed, and Robby quickly shot the ball back.

But James's hands weren't there to take it. He had pulled away too quickly.

The ball ticked off James's fingertips and fell to the ground. "Fumble!" someone yelled. The players scrambled for the ball, and the Cowboys got it.

Robby was the last one up when the pile cleared. When he reached the sideline, the coach grabbed him by the jersey.

"Samuels!" he screamed. "What the heck happened out there?" Robby knew he hadn't made the mistake this time.

Robby looked at James. James had his head down, but he didn't say a word.

"I don't know what happened," Robby said.

Chapter 10

BIGGER CHANGES

The game ended in a 14–14 tie. After the players from both teams shook hands, Coach Parker got the Lions in a circle around him. Coach Parker took a deep breath. "I didn't work you guys hard enough," he said. "This week, we'll do an extra hour of practice each day."

The next three nights of practice were brutal. The coach ran the boys through drill after drill. They ran extra sprints every time they made a mistake.

Their next game was on a Saturday afternoon against the Rams. When Robby got to the field, James was already taking snaps from another player. As Robby stepped closer to James, Coach Parker called to him. "Samuels! You're working with the defense."

The defense? Robby was stunned, but he did what he was told. As a defensive tackle, he worked on his stance, on his tackling, and on fighting off blocks. The whole time, however, he wondered why he was not playing center.

When the game started, David Brownfield was playing center. Robby was on the bench. When the Lions went on defense, Robby took turns with another player on the defensive line.

At halftime, Robby saw Matt. He
raised his arms, like he was asking,
What's up? Robby shrugged.

In the second half, Robby stayed on
defense. The Rams won easily, 35–12.

After the game, Robby and Matt walked home.

"I went from playing every play on offense to only playing half of the plays on defense," Robby said.

"Maybe he just doesn't know how good you can be on defense," Matt said.

"Maybe he just doesn't like me," Robby shot back.

The boys were quiet for a while. Finally, Matt said, "Well, it could be worse. You could be the water boy."

The boys laughed.

Chapter 11

END OF A LONG SEASON

Things didn't get better for the Lions. The tie in the first game of the season was the best they had done. With only one game left, their record was zero wins, eight losses, one tie. Worse yet, the Lions were losing by two or three touchdowns every game.

Robby started working harder on defense. As defensive tackle, he was usually lined up against the other team's center.

Since he had played center before, he knew what the other player was thinking.

He got better as the season went on. He just didn't feel like a part of the team.

Finally, the last game arrived. The Saints were sitting in fourth place. They knew that one more win would put them in the playoffs. That made Robby worry. Since the Saints had good reason to play hard, and the Lions didn't, Robby thought his team might get beat badly.

Before the opening kickoff, Coach Parker gathered the players around him. "We can still do something with this season," he said. "We might not win the championship, but we can still end our season with a win!"

Robby was pumped up. But he was a little shocked by how excited everyone else was to play.

The game got off to a great start. James made a long run on the first play. Andy had a couple of good runs too. Finally, they got the ball down inside the Saints' ten-yard line.

On first down, Andy plowed through the middle but only gained one yard. There was a big pile of players in the middle of the field. As they got up, one player stayed on the ground.

It was David Brownfield. He was holding his ankle. Robby popped up. He knew what this might mean — a chance to play center again. Coach Parker helped David off the field.

"Okay, Samuels, you're in," Coach Parker said.

Robby charged out onto the field. "Oh, great," Andy said. "Here comes trouble."

"Shut up, Andy," Robby said. The whole team shot a glance at Robby. Even Robby was surprised it came out of him. "Do you want to win or not?"

No one said a word, not even James. Robby looked at the ball. It was on the three-yard line. "Let's run that twenty-two power drive play," Robby said. James looked at him. "Andy, we'll get the hole open. You push it through. Okay?"

"Um, okay," Andy said.

"On two," James said. A confident smile crossed his face. "Twenty-two power drive on two."

The team broke the huddle and charged to the line. Robby was about to burst. He couldn't wait to snap that ball and hit the defensive tackle. He didn't know what was making him so confident, but he liked it.

James called out the signals. "Hut! Hut!" Robby snapped the ball straight into James's hands. James spun and shoved the ball into Andy's belly. Robby drove straight ahead and plowed the defensive tackle aside. The hole opened, and Andy went straight through it, into the end zone.

The Lions had the lead! Robby traded highfives with the other linemen. Andy and James jumped up and bumped chests.

When they got to the sideline after the extra point, Robby smacked Andy on the back. "Nice run," Robby said. Andy looked back. "Yeah," he said, turning away.

The Saints weren't going to let the game slip away, however. They tied the game with a touchdown. Then the Saints took a 14–7 lead into halftime.

"Samuels," Coach Parker said, "You're the man in the second half. You showed some good leadership out there. Keep it up."

"Thanks," Robby said, smiling.

Chapter 12

BIG FINISH

Before the second half started, Robby gathered the rest of the linemen around him. "Okay, guys," he said. "If we all do our jobs, we can beat this team. Let's go out there and do it!"

Starting on their twelve-yard line, the Lions began to drive down the field. After each run, Robby smacked the ball carrier on the back and told him, "Nice run."

Finally, the Lions had a fourth down on the Saints' nineteen-yard line. James took the snap and pitched it to Andy. Andy started to the right. Then he saw a Saints' player coming straight at him. There was no one to block him. Andy tried to stop, but he slipped. When Andy got his balance back, he turned left, running as fast as he could.

But the defender was on him, just a step away. Robby pushed away from the tackle and charged into the backfield. Just as the defender was about to reach Andy, Robby dove and hit the defender's shoulder. Both players fell to the ground.

Now Andy was free. He strolled into the end zone easily.

Robby stood up to see Andy cross the goal line, raising his hands.

Robby had never felt anything like it. He had saved the play.

The game was tied 14–14. As the players reached the sideline, Robby went over to Andy. "Hey, nice escape," Robby laughed.

Andy looked at him, not sure of what to say. Finally, he said, "Not bad, Samuels. Not bad."

Robby knew it was Andy's way of saying thanks.

With less than a minute to play, the Lions were back inside the Saints' ten-yard line. A touchdown would win the game.

The players wanted to do anything just to get that zero off their record.

Coach Parker called the first-down play. It was a run for Andy.

Robby bent over the ball and snapped it to James. James turned and handed the ball to Andy.

A defensive player's hand shot out and caught a piece of Andy's sleeve, and another player slammed into him. "Ahhh!" Andy shouted. Then Robby saw it. The ball was falling to the ground. Without thinking, Robby dove for it. Players piled on, but Robby got there first. He felt the ball against his chest.

"I got it!" he yelled. "It's still ours!"

When the officials got the players off the pile, Robby handed the ball to the referee. He turned back toward the huddle.

Andy held out his hand. Robby reached over and gave him five.

"Thanks, man," Andy said.

"One more play to go," Robby said.

Coach Parker called the twenty-two power drive play. Robby helped open a big hole, and Andy ran straight through it for the game-winning touchdown.

The Lions acted like they had won the championship. They jumped around, slapping hands and bumping chests.

Just then, Andy walked over to Robby. He had a big grin on his face, not the smirk Robby was used to seeing.

"Hey, Samuels," Andy said. "Nice job. You saved my butt today."

Robby couldn't believe what he was hearing.

"We're a team," Robby said. Robby held out his hand, and Andy gave him five.

Finally, Coach Parker gathered all the boys around him. "Well, boys," he said. "We may not have won the championship, but we played like champions today!"

All the boys cheered.

About the Author

Bob Temple lives in Rosemount, Minnesota, with his wife and three children. He has written more than thirty books for children. Over the years, he has coached more than twenty kids' soccer, basketball, and baseball teams. He also loves visiting classrooms to talk about his writing.

About the Illustrator

When Sean Tiffany was growing up, he lived on a small island off the coast of Maine. Every day, from sixth grade until he graduated from high school, he had to take a boat to get to school. When Sean isn't working on his art, he works on a multimedia project called "OilCan Drive," which combines music and art. He has a pet cactus named Jim.

Glossary

confident (KON-fuh-dent)—feeling sure of your abilities

crouch (KROWCH)—to bend down low

fumbled (FUM-buld)—dropped

huddle (HUD-dul)—a group of people standing close together

penalty (PEN-ul-tee)—a punishment for breaking the rules

referee (ref-uh-REE)—a person who watches a sports game to make sure that all players follow the rules

sarcastically (sar-KASS-tik-lee)—spoken in a teasing or mocking way

scrimmage (SKRIM-idj)—a sports game played for practice

stance (STANSS)—a position or way of standing

Offense and Defense

The offense is the name for the team who carries the ball. The offense tries to get a touchdown.

The center starts each offensive play. He snaps the ball to the quarterback. Then the quarterback hands the ball to the running back or throws it to a receiver.

Linebackers try to tackle and block the players of the other team. They don't want the other team to catch the ball or wreck the play.

The defense plays against the offense. The defensive players try to tackle, block, and catch the other team's passes. They do this to keep the other team from scoring.

Discussion Questions

1. At the beginning of the story, Robby was afraid to go back on the football field. Why did he feel this way?

2. When James fumbled the football, Robby took the blame. Why didn't Robby say anything to the coach? What might have happened if Robby blamed the mistake on James?

3. Why did Robby's attitude change by the end of the story?

Writing Prompts

1. At the end of the story, Andy thanked Robby for saving the play. Write about a time when someone who was mean to you changed. Why do you think the person changed?

2. Describe your favorite character in the story. Now describe your least favorite character. Explain how they are the same and how they are different.

3. List some ways to deal with bullies. Then list some of the things Robby did to deal with Andy. Did Robby's methods work?

Internet Sites

Do you want to know more about subjects related to this book? Or are you interested in learning about other topics? Then check out FactHound, a fun, easy way to find Internet sites.

Our investigative staff has already sniffed out great sites for you!

Here's how to use FactHound:

1. Visit *www.facthound.com*

2. Select your grade level.

3. To learn more about subjects related to this book, type in the book's ISBN number: **159889062X**.

4. Click the **Fetch It** button.

FactHound will fetch the best Internet sites for you!